LITTLE TRICKER THE SQUIRREL

MEETS BIG DOUBLE THE BEAR

LITTLE TRICKER
The Squirrel

MEETS BIG DOUBLE

the Bear

by Ken Kesey

Illustrated by Barry Moser

PUFFIN BOOKS

For Grandma Smith
still lighting the dark—K.K.

For Jane, Tom, Brooke & Cecily
—B.M.

PUFFIN BOOKS
Published by the Penguin Group
Penguin Books USA Inc., 375 Hudson Street, New York, New York 10014, U.S.A.
Penguin Books Ltd, 27 Wrights Lane, London W8 5TZ, England
Penguin Books Australia Ltd, Ringwood, Victoria, Australia
Penguin Books Canada Ltd, 10 Alcorn Avenue, Toronto, Ontario, Canada M4V 3B2
Penguin Books (N.Z.) Ltd, 182–190 Wairau Road, Auckland 10, New Zealand

Penguin Books Ltd, Registered Offices: Harmondsworth, Middlesex, England

First published in the United States of America by Viking Penguin,
a division of Penguin Books USA Inc., 1990
Published in Puffin Books, 1992

1 3 5 7 9 10 8 6 4 2

Text copyright © Ken Kesey, 1990
Illustrations copyright © Pennyroyal Press, Inc., 1990
All rights reserved

This story previously appeared in different form in *Wonders* (Straight
Arrow Press) and Mr. Kesey's *Demon Box* (Viking Penguin).

LIBRARY OF CONGRESS CATALOGING-IN-PUBLICATION DATA
Kesey, Ken.
Little Tricker the squirrel meets Big Double the bear / by Ken
Kesey; illustrated by Barry Moser.   p. cm.
Summary: Little Tricker the squirrel watches as Big Double the
bear terrorizes the forest animals one by one,
but then Little Tricker gets revenge.
ISBN 0-14-050623-3
[1. Animals—Fiction.]   I. Moser, Barry, ill.   II. Title.
PZ7.K4814Li 1992   [E]—dc20   92-10605

Printed in Japan
Set in Sabon

LITTLE TRICKER THE SQUIRREL
MEETS BIG DOUBLE THE BEAR

ON'T TELL ME YOU'RE the *only* youngsters never heard tell of the time the bear came to Topple's Bottom? He was a huge high-country bear and not only huge but *horrible* huge. And hairy, and hateful, and *hungry!* Why, he almost ate up the *entire Bottom* before Tricker finally cut him down to size, just you listen and see if he didn't. . . .

It was a fine fall morning, early and cold and sweet as cider. Down in the Bottom the only one up and about was old Papa Sun, and him just barely. Hanging in the low limbs of the crab-apple trees was still some of those strings of daybreak fog called "haint hair" by them that believes in such. The night shifts and the day shifts were shifting very slow. The crickets hadn't put away their fiddles. The spiders hadn't shook the dew out of their webs yet. The birds hadn't quite woke up and the bats hadn't quite gone to sleep. Nothing was a-move except one finger of sun slipping soft up the knobby trunk of the hazel. It was one of the prettiest times of the day at one of the prettiest times of the year, and all the Bottom folk were content to let it come about quiet and slow and savory.

Tricker the Squirrel was awake but he wasn't about. He was lazying in the highest hole in his cottonwood high rise with just his nose poking from his pillow of a tail, dreaming about flying. Every now and again he would twinkle one bright eye out through his dream and his puffy pillow-hair to check the hazel tree way down below to see if any of the nuts were ready for reaping. He had to admit they were all pretty near prime. All day yesterday he had watched those nuts turning softly browner and browner and, come sundown, had judged them just one day short of perfect.

"And *that* means if I don't get them today, to*morrow* they are very apt to be just one day *past* perfect."

So he was promising himself, "Just as quick as that sunbeam touches that first hazelnut I get right on the job." And then, after a couple of winks, "Just as quick as that sunbeam touches the *second* hazelnut I'll zip right down with my tote sack and go to gathering,"—and so forth, merely dozing and dallying, and savoring the sweet, still air. The hazelnuts get browner. The sunbeam inches silently on—to the *fif*teenth! the *twen*tieth!—but the morning was simply so pretty and the air hanging so dreamy and still he hated to break the peace.

Well, then, the finger just about touches the twenty-*sev*enth hazelnut, when a holy dad-blamed gosh-almighty *roar* came kabooming through the Bottom like a freight druv by the Devil himself, or at least his next hottest hollerer.

Oh, what a roar! Oh, oh, *oh!* And not just loud and long, but high and low and chilling and fiery all to once. The haint hair and the spider webs all froze stiff—it was *that chilling!*—whilst the springs boiled dry and the crab apples burned black from the hell-heat of it. Even way up in Tricker's tall, tall tree the cottonwood leaves turned brown and looked ready to fall still *weeks* before their time. Moreover, that roar had startled Tricker out of his snooze so sudden that he *stuck startled,* halfway between the ceiling and the floor. And hung there, petrified, spraddle-eagled spellbound stiff in midair, with eyes big as biscuits and every hair stabbing straight out from him like quills on a puffed-up porcupine!

"*What* in the name of *sixty cyclones* was *that?*" he asks himself in a quakering voice. "A dream gone nightmare?"

He pinches his nose to check. The spellbind busts and Tricker drops hard to the floor: *bump!*

"Hmm," he puzzles, rubbing his nose and his knees, "it *is* like a dream with a little nightmare noise thrown in—like a plain old floating and flying *dream* dream . . . except! when you get real bumps it must be a real floor."

And right then it cut loose again—"ROAWRRR!" shaking the cottonwood from root to crown till a critter could hardly stand. Tricker crawls cautious across the floor on his sore knees, and very cautious sticks his sore nose out, and very *very* cautious cranes over to look way down into the clearing below.

"Again I say ROAWRR!"

The sound made Tricker's ears ring and his blood curdle, and the sight he saw made him wonder if he wasn't still dreaming, bumps or no.

"I'm BIG DOUBLE from the high wild ridges, and I'm DOUBLE BIG and I'm DOUBLE BAD and I'm DOUBLE DOUBLE HONGRY a-ROARRR!"

It was a bear, a *grizz*erly bear, so big and hairy and horrible it looked like the two biggest baddest bears in the Ozarks had teamed up to make one.

"Again I says, HONGRY! And I don't mean lunchtime snacktime littletime hongry, I mean grumpy grouchy bedtime *big*time hongry. I live big, I sleep big. And when I hit the hay tonight I got six months before breakfast so I need a supper the size of my sleep. I need a *big* bellyfull of fuel and lay-by of fat to fire my full-time furnace and stoke my six-months snore a-ROOAAHRRRR!"

When the bear opened his mouth his teeth looked like stalactites

in a cavern. When his tummy rumbled it sounded like thunder in the faraway hills. And when he swung his head around, his eyes looked like a double-barrel shotgun shooting shooting stars.

"I ate the high hills bare as a *bone* and the foothills raw as a *rock,* and now I'm going to eat the WHOLE! BOTTOM! and everybody in it ALL . . . UP!"

And with that gives another *aw*ful roar and raises his paws high above his head, stretching till his toenails strain out like so many shiny sharp hay hooks, then rams *down!* sinking them claws clean outta sight into the *ground*. And with an evil snarl tears the very earth wide open like it was so much wrapping paper on his birthday present.

In the sundered earth there was Charlie Charles the Woodchuck, his bedroom split half in two, his bedstead busted beneath him and his bedspread pulled up to his quivering chin.

"Hey, you," Charlie demands, in the bravest voice the little fella can muster, "this is *my* hole! What are you doing breaking into my home and hole?"

"Well, I'm BIG DOUBLE from the HIGH WILD HOLLERS, son," the bear snarls, "and I'm loading the old larder up for one of my DOUBLE LONG WINTER NAPS."

"Well, just you go larding up someplace else, you high hills hol-lerer," Charlie snarls back. "This ain't *your* neck of the woods. . . ."

"Son, when I'm hongry it's ALLLL Big Double's neck of the

woods!" says the bear. "And I'M HONNNGRY. I ate the HIGH HILLS RAW and the FOOTHILLS BARE and now I'm going to EAT! YOU! UP!"

"I'll run," says the woodchuck, glaring his most glittering glare.

"I can run *too*-oo," says the bear, glaring back with a grin that turns poor Charlie's glitter to gloom. Charlie meets the bear's blistering stare for a couple ticks more, and then *out* from under the covers he springs and *out* acrost the Bottom he tears, ears laid low, tail hoisted high, and little feet hitting the ground sixty-six steps a second . . . *fast!*

But the big old bear with his big old feet merely takes one! two! three! double-big steps, and takes Charlie over, and snags him up, and swallers him down, hair, hide, and *whole*sale.

High up in his hole Tricker blinks his eyes in amazement. "Yep," he has to allow, "that big booger really can run."

The bear then walks down the hill to the big granite boulder by the creek where Longrellers the Rabbit lived. He listens a moment, his ear to the stone, then lifts one of those size fifty feet as high as his double-big legs can hoist it, lifted like a huge hairy pile driver, and with one stomp turns poor Longrellers's granite fortress into a sandpile all over the rabbit's breakfast table.

"You Ozark clodhopper!" Longrellers squeals, trying to dig the sand out of one of his long ears with a wild parsnip. "This is *my* breakfast, not yours. You've got a nerve, come stomping down here

into our Bottom, busting up our property and our privacy. This ain't *even* your stomping grounds!"

"I hate to tell you, cousin, but I'm BIG DOUBLE and ALLLL the ground I stomp on is mine. I ate the high hills BARE and the foothills CLEAN. I ate the woodchuck that run and now I'm going to EAT! YOU! UP!"

"I'll run," says the rabbit.

"I can run *too*-oo," says the bear.

"I'll jump," says the rabbit.

"I can jump *too*-oo," says the bear, grinning and glaring and wiggling his whiskers wickedly at the rabbit. Longrellers wiggles his whiskers back a couple of ticks, and then *out* across the territory rips the rabbit, a cloud of sand boiling up from his heels like dust from a motor scooter scooting up a steep dirt road. But right after him comes the bear, like a loaded log train coming down a steeper one. Longrellers is almost to the hedge at the edge of the Topple pasture when he gathers his long ears and his elbows under him and he jumps for the brambles, springing up into the air quick as a quail flushing . . . fast, and *far!*

But the big old bear with his big old legs springs after him like a rocket ship roaring, and takes the rabbit over at the peak of his jump, and snags him up, and swallers him down, ears, elbows, and every-thing.

"Good as his word the big bum can certainly jump," admits Tricker, watching bug-eyed from his high bedroom window.

Next, the bear goes down to where Whittier Crick is dribbling drowsy by. He grabs the crick by its bank and with one wicked snap, snaps it like a bedspread. This snaps Sally Snipsister the Marten clear out of her mud-burrow boudoir and her toenail polish, summersetting her into the air over and over, and then lands her hard in the emptied creek bed along with stunned mud puppies and minnows.

"You backwoods bully!" Sally hisses. "You ridge-running rowdy! What are you doing down out of your ridges ripping up our rivers? This isn't your play puddle!"

"Why, ma'am, I'm Big Double and ANY puddle I please to play in is mine. I ate the ridges *raw* and the backwoods *bald*. I ate the woodchuck that run and I ate the rabbit that jumped. And now I'm going to EAT! YOU! UP!"

"I'll run," says the marten.

"I can run *too*-oo," says the bear.

"I'll jump," says the marten.

"I can jump *too*-oo," says the bear.

"I'll climb," says the marten.

"I can climb *too*-oo," says the bear, and champs his big yellow choppers in a challenging chomp. Sally clicks back at him with her own sharp little teeth for a tick or two, click-click-click . . . then *off*

she shoots like the bullet out of a pistol. But right after her booms the bear like a meteor out of a cannon. Sally springs out of the creek bed like a silver salmon jumping. The bear jumps after her like a flying shark. She catches the trunk of the cottonwood and climbs like an electric yo-yo whizzing up a wire. But the bear climbs after her like a jet-propelled elevator up a greasy groove, and takes her over, and snags her up, and swallers her down, teeth, toenails, and teetotal.

And then, it so happens, while the big bear is hugging the tree and licking his lips, he sees! that he is eye-to-eye with a little hole that is none other than the door of the bedroom of Tricker the Squirrel.

"Yessiree bob," Tricker has to concede. "You also sure as shooting can *climb*."

"WHO are YOU?" roars the bear.

"I'm Tricker the Squirrel, and I saw it all. And there's just no two ways about it: I'm impressed—you may have been a little short-changed in the thinking department but when it comes to running, jumping, and climbing you got double portions."

"And EAT!" roars the bear into the hole. "I'm BIG DOUBLE and I ate—"

"I know, I know," says Tricker, his fingers in his ears. "The ridges raw and the hills bare. I *heard* it all, too."

"And NOW I'm going to EAT—"

"You're gonna eat me up, I know," groans Tricker. "But first I'm gonna *run,* right?"

"And I'm gonna run *too*-oo," says the bear.

"Then I'm gonna *jump,*" says Tricker.

"And I'm gonna jump *too*-oo," says the bear.

"Then I'm gonna *drink some buttermilk,*" says Tricker.

"I'm . . . gonna drink buttermilk *too*-oo," says the bear.

"Then I'm gonna *climb,*" says Tricker.

"And I'm gonna climb *too*-oo," says the bear.

"And *then,*" says Tricker, smiling and winking and plucking at one of his longest whiskers dainty as a riverboat gambler with a sleeve full of secrets, "I am going to *fly!*"

This bamboozles the bear, and for a second he furrows his big brow. But everybody—even short-changed grizzerly bears named Big Double—*knows* red squirrels can't fly . . . not even red squirrels named Tricker.

"Well, then," says the bear, grinning and winking and plucking at one of his own longest whitest whiskers with a big clumsy claw, "when *you* fly, I'll fly *too*-oo."

"We'll *see*-ee about that," says Tricker and, without a word or wink more, reaches over to jerk the bear's whisker *clean out.* UhroAWRRR! roars the bear and he makes a nab, but Tricker is *out* the hole and streaking down the tree trunk like a bolt of greased

lightning with the bear thundering right behind him, meaner and madder than ever. Tricker streaks across the Bottom toward the Topple farm with the bear storming right on his tail. When he reaches the milk house where Farmer Topple cools his dairy products he jumps right through the window. The bear jumps right through after him. Tricker hops up on the edge of a gallon crock and begins to guzzle up the cool, thick buttermilk like he hadn't had a sip of liquid for a month.

The bear knocks him aside and picks up the whole crock and sucks it down like he was a seven-year drought.

Tricker then hops up to the rim of the *five*-gallon crock and starts to lap up the buttermilk.

But the bear knocks him aside again, and hefts the crock and drinks it down.

Tricker doesn't even bother hopping to the brim of the last crock, a *ten*-galloner. He just stands back dodging the drops while the bear heaves the vessel high, tips it up, and, gradually, *guzz*les it empty.

The bear finally plunks down the last crock, and he wipes his chops and he roars, "I'm BIG DOUBLE and I ate the HIGH HILLS—"

"I know, I know," says Tricker, wincing. "Let's skip the roaring and get right on to the last part, okay? After I run, and jump, and drink buttermilk, then I *climb*."

"I climb *too*-erp," says the bear, belching.

"And I fly," says Tricker.

"And I fly *too*-up," says the bear, hiccupping.

So *back* out of the milk house jumps Tricker and *off* he goes, dusting back toward the cottonwood like a baby dust-devil, with the bear huffing right at his heels like a full-blown tornado. And *up* the tree he scorches like a house afire, with the bear right on his tail like a volcano. Higher and higher climbs Tricker, with the bear's hot breath huffing hotter and hotter, and closer and closer, and higher and higher, till there's *bare*ly any tree left . . . and then *out* into the fine fall air Tricker springs, like a little red leaf light on the wind.

And—before the bear thinks better of it—*out* he springs hisself, like a ten-ton milk tanker over the edge of a cliff.

"I forgot to *men*tion," Tricker sings out as he grabs the leafy top of that first sun-touched hazelnut tree and hangs there, swinging and swaying: "I can also *trick*."

"ARGGHHH!" his pursuer answers, plummeting right past, "AAARRggh—" *all* the way, till he splatters on the hillside like a thumping ripe melon.

When the dust and debris clear back, Sally Snipsister wriggles up from the wrecked remains and says, "I'm out!"

Then Longrellers the Rabbit jumps up and says, "I'm out!"

Then Charlie Charles the Woodchuck pops up and says, "I'm out!"

"I," says Tricker, swinging high in the sunny branches where the hazelnuts are *just about per*fect, "was never in to *get* out."

And everybody laughed, and the birds woke up and commenced to sing, and the hazelnuts got more and more perfect, and the buttermilk just rolled . . .

        down . . .

            the hill.

The art for *Little Tricker the Squirrel Meets Big Double the Bear* was painted with transparent watercolors on handmade papers prepared for the Royal Watercolor Society by Simon Green, and by the Fabriano Mills, Fabriano Italy.